Mairead O'Driscoll was born in Co. Offaly and now lives in Midleton, Co. Cork, with her husband Leonard. She works as a Public Health Nurse with the HSE. *Where the Heart is* is her third novel. She has written *Absolute Beginners* and *Pebble Cove,* also published by Poolbeg.

www.maireadodriscoll.com

Acknowledgements

It is with enormous gratitude that I acknowledge the contribution made by so many to the publication of *Where the Heart is*.

As ever, it is Len who has kept the show on the road from beginning to end with a constant supply of love, encouragement and understanding.

To Mam, Dad and all the gang at home, as always, thank you for all the support in the past few years – your love and attention is appreciated every single day.

To my mother-in-law, Nonie – thank you for everything.

To my friends, who know already what they mean to me – you are irreplaceable as well as being great fun.

To my agent, Ger Nichol, for her support and understanding.

To all at Poolbeg, especially Paula Campbell, Niamh Fitzgerald and Gaye Shortland for your patience, hard work and for making my dream come true yet again.

To my fantastic colleagues (present and past) at Midleton Health Centre for your unstinting loyalty and great company.

To Jess, Ronan, Aisling and all at Midleton Books for being part of this exciting journey – your support has been invaluable and much appreciated.

To the most important people ever – the readers who have plucked *Pebble Cove* and *Absolute Beginners* off the shelves and made the characters become real in the best way possible. Thank you to all the readers who've taken the time to write and email – it means the world to me to know you have enjoyed my work.

Once again, my wonderful Len, thank you for walking beside me and being my friend. I love you more than I can say.

As always, for Lenny.
My friend, my second self.

"Love you to bits."

Chapter 1

Emily Gordon closed the back door quietly so that her mother wouldn't hear her leaving the house. The last thing she needed was an audience, however supportive. She set off down the road, glad that the village was reasonably quiet for her reconnaissance mission.

Rathmollin was a passing-through village, often described as "starting at one end and finishing at the other". Apart from the few cars racing along the main street on their way to somewhere other than Rathmollin, the place was quiet. Just as well, considering that her innocuous stroll would probably be the talk of the place if she was spotted by Aggie Lenihan, the local gossip. As it stood, Emily reckoned that she'd provided Aggie with quite enough mileage for one year and wasn't prepared to offer any more of her life up as a sacrifice to her hobby. She'd already answered more than her fair share of "innocent" questions about The Wedding that Never Was.

Apart from a large extension to the rear and a line of

three neat prefabs along one side of the yard, St Ciaran's primary school looked much as it had the day Emily first walked through its front door at the age of five. It had only been a matter of months before she'd broken a little hole in the hedge that divided her parents' house from the school and after that the yard had become like an extension of her own home. Her parents had tolerated the gap as it allowed Emily and her brother to go to school without having to incur the risks of the main road. It was still there.

The school door was painted red now and the front windows were overflowing with a profusion of petunias and lobelias in heavy terracotta containers. Even at this hour, six o'clock on a Sunday evening, there was someone there. She could hear the rhythmic grate of gravel being shovelled and wondered what new project the Parents' Council had on the burner.

Harmony Cottage was at the far end of the village. Having spent the better part of the day just lying on her bed, the short walk would actually do her good. Something about the badly focused photo of the little house in *The Examiner* had made her feel as if she might actually have a future, not a bad thing considering that up to now she hadn't been able to see anything past a black hole when tomorrow or next week or next year was mentioned.

She walked on, past Curly Locks hair salon, Connolly's Master Butcher and Mac Gleeson's Grocery, her hair blowing away from her face in the blustery March wind. Richard used to love the feeling of her unruly auburn ringlets tickling his face when they were out walking, or at least that's what he'd said at the time. Emily wasn't sure now what had been true and what had been a lie but at least she was beginning to wonder about it less and less.

She was nearing the cottage now and was almost starting to feel scared that it would be a disappointment in real life. She knew how the property pages could pump up a house so that it was the Taj Mahal you were expecting by the time you viewed it.

She could just imagine what Richard would say if he knew she was considering a house that was probably a hundred years old but it was a bit late now to be worrying about what *his* advice and opinions might be. Maybe a shift away from a state-of-the-art, all-mod-cons show-house was what she needed right now. And, thanks to Richard, that was just about all she could afford.

Emily lifted her chin in the manner that she'd learned to adopt since that fateful moment on New Year's Eve and strode purposefully towards what she hoped might be her fresh start.

Sandra Coyne was glad of the excuse of picking up Dylan's bike from the pathway outside her parents' house and for the feeling of the fresh air on her face. Her father had been on at her about Paul again and she was finding it more and more difficult to defend him, especially when it was gone six o'clock and she'd had no account of him since lunch-time.

New Year's Eve had been wonderful, an emotional if somewhat drunken reunion with the father of her child, her first great love. Her only great love, come to think of it, considering that she'd barely been out of the house in the last eight years. Now, over three months on, Sandra wasn't so sure.

She and Paul had made a pact to put the past behind them and start again and she'd truly wanted to let bygones be bygones and start from scratch for Dylan's sake. As Paul had pointed out on New Year's Eve, Dylan had a right to know his father and Sandra knew it wasn't fair of her to deny him that.

And despite everything, as soon as she saw him again in The Stone's Throw, the old familiar attraction had come back to her as if the intervening years had never happened. She'd always loved the height of him – the way he towered over her made her feel somehow cherished, like a china doll next to his muscled bulk. The wide grin and bright blue eyes that were now so familiar in her son reminded her that they used to be a family and could be again if she let it happen. But it was the comforting weight of his arm where it rested across her shoulder that night that had made her believe it was possible to start again, that and the way he made her laugh with tales of his life in London. A life that he was prepared to leave for another chance with Sandra and Dylan.

He'd been happy to move into the small council house opposite the school with them and had been raring to go when Sandra mentioned to Jack Rooney the following Saturday night that Paul would be looking for work. They'd had a drink together in The Stone's that night and Jack had been happy for Paul to start the following Monday.

It had been great those first few weeks, a honeymoon period that had given her a new lease of life. Somehow, though, the shine had worn off a bit. The ritual of daily life was getting harder and she was beginning to wonder if she'd made a mistake in rushing into things with Paul once again.

It wasn't the first time that he'd let her down, her father had warned her a few minutes ago. He knew that Paul spent more time in The Stone's than was strictly sociable, but what he didn't know was how easy it was to irritate him when he came home late and how his drinking was eating into Sandra's already tight budget. It was all very fine saying "I told you so", but in actual fact nobody *had* told her so. It was up to her now to make the best of it, for Dylan's sake if not her own.

She leaned against the front wall, reluctant to go back inside and face more of her parents' weary disapproval. Then a huddled figure walking towards her caught her attention – a chance perhaps to delay the inevitable return inside.

"Emily!"

It had been ages since she'd spoken to Emily Gordon. Sandra knew from her mother that an engagement had been dissolved in the last few months but it would be the last thing she'd mention – unless of course Emily herself brought it up.

"God, Sandra, I was dreaming there – I hardly noticed you. How are you?"

Emily looked pale, but then she'd always had an ethereal sort of look. The creamy skin (its light sprinkling of freckles well concealed) and dark auburn curls had always reminded Sandra of the kind of paintings that had naked ladies and cherubs in them.

"Great. Just tidying up after Dylan – he's a terror for leaving things all over the place."

"He must be big now. Eight?"

Emily had a way of screwing her face up that made Sandra feel old in comparison.

"Next week. I can't believe it. Are you home for a bit?" As far as she knew, Emily was still working in Dublin.

"For the moment. I'm working in Cork now so I'm starting to look for my own place."

"Any luck? The new ones over the road look nice."

"Expensive though – they're all well over three hundred thousand."

They both glanced across the road to where the stone entrance of Sycamore Drive was blocked off for the night by a strategically placed excavator.

"I actually came up along to have a look at Ina Harrington's cottage. I saw it in *The Examiner* yesterday."

To Sandra, the rundown cottage was little better than the small council house that she herself was renting at the other end of the village and she was surprised that Emily was even thinking about it, considering that she had a college education and a good job as a social worker.

"I noticed it was for sale," she said. "Would it need much work, do you think?"

"I've no idea. It's worth looking at though."

Sandra wasn't sure that it was but couldn't exactly say so to Emily who was gazing towards Ina and her sister Minnie's old cottage with a wistful look in her eyes. Besides, to Sandra, the idea of owning her own home was as far from reality as flying to the moon and she envied